Beyond the Curve…

Short Stories

By

Eddie J. Martin

Contents

When Billie Holiday sang about "Strange Fruits" I didn't know what she meant—wasn't about fruits at all.

John Chandler and Centrale are back to clean up Chicago in their own style. Chicago will never be the same.

She could have had it all; she should have seen it coming.

Treat people like you would like to be treated, love the ones

who love you, and never take it for granted.

You give a person everything she ever wanted, everything she ever

had, and still she wants more; nothing else you can do now but kill

her ass.

Is it true what they say about male virgins?

 High school girls devised a plan to molest

all the virgin males on a bet.

A hit of heroin, a trick that pays twice, a coworker offering a place to

stay. It doesn't get any better than that, can it?

When you're young, you never know what you're looking for, what you'll find; the unexpected, mostly.

Sometimes you wonder who's the predator and who's not. You'd be surprised.

PROLOGUE

After you reached a certain age in your life, there is this urge to go back to your birthplace, as I did, to see the places you grew up and wonder if the places you remember are still there, still the same. The creek that you went fishing and swimming in; do the mountains still look the same? Do the lightning bugs still come out at night? you wonder. So I went back.

MY NAME IS Maxwell Cleaver. At age 68, I just retired from my job at J. R. Electric Company after 35 years. I did six years with the military and various other jobs, and ended up as a salesman, which took me all over the world. Japan, Korea, Europe, and Australia. China and Russia, and all over this United States. Driving, taking trains or planes . . . it's been a hell of a career and I've loved every minute of it. I was married half of those years, but due to differences we got divorced, but we're still friends.

I don't know where I got the idea of going back to my birthplace; never thought about home before. I never lost anything back there, so why in the hell was I wanting to go back at this stage of my life? I'm from the hills of Kentucky, Pike County. If you haven't heard of that part of the country, think of the Hatfields and the McCoys that's been fighting there for about 100 years.

My family left when I was eight. Over the years I thought about my home, as anyone would, I guess. You see things as you remember them and deep down you think they'll be the same when you see them again, but they never are.

The places I have been in the country; I've always been amazed at how the area had changed once I saw them again. New building versus the old, streets restored, and homes totally removed or remodeled. But then, after 30 to 40 years, it's still a bit shocking. Once I went back to where I used to be stationed when I was in the military. At that time there were few people and you had room to breathe, like a small town you'd see in a Norman Rockwell picture. Slow, slow! Drive for miles and see little or no traffic. Walk down the street and you had running room. Even off the base you knew quite a few people in town, nice! But you didn't know all this at the time. Now 40 years later . . . people on top of people, vehicles on top of vehicles. The old hangouts I remember are totally gone. Not only that, the town that I remembered was nothing but a truck stop. Who would have thunk it. But then, that's progress. Even the highways are turning into freeways.

I made my way to the river. I knew that was still there. It was.

I decided to drive to Kentucky from Texas, do a little sightseeing. Didn't count on having an accident along the way, but things happen. I killed two to three days waiting in Cleveland, Tennessee, to see what the insurance company was going to do; a waste of time, really. Glad I didn't have a job to go back to; now I have nothing but time to burn and money to do it with.

That night after the accident, I asked where I could find a place to eat besides fast food. I was told that right behind the motel was a Cracker Barrel restaurant, and I went there. Before going in, I stood around to see if any of us (blacks) were going in or coming out. Even at my age and the places I've been, you still have to be careful, especially if you're black.

Next day, I headed up the road to Kentucky and the Appalachian Mountains. The only thing I ran into on the way was more rain.

I knew I was getting close; never saw this many Confederate flags, even in Texas. And with the road constantly going up and up, I was thinking this place was going to be somewhere near the moon. At first I passed right by the turnoff, but there was no sign saying McVeigh or any other town so I drove right into Williamson, West Virginia, the closest town to McVeigh, as I remember it.

It looked like the other places I had visited, much like many of the places I've been. Last time I was here they had one main street; I remember that because that's where I got hit by a car. The person who witnessed the accident said I was bouncing like a rubber ball underneath. Bullshit! Or I always thought it was.

Now it looks like a real town; fast-food restaurants all over the place and liquor stores, traffic up the ass. I figured I had driven too far so I asked around to see if anyone knew of a small town named McVeigh. The two white guys in the parking lot of the library hooking up to the library's Wi-Fi started giving me directions how to get there, and just as I figured, I had passed right by the turnoff. Then they asked me why in the hell I would ever want to go there, there's not a damn thing there except snakes and Klansmen. They were in disbelief; no one ever goes there, that place is the pits. Then I told them that I was born there and I just wanted to see how it had changed, or not changed. They told me to turn left and go through two little towns, then after the second town there'd be an oil supply company in the middle of the street so I'd have to go around it, since the street split at that point. Take the left turn. If I went right, I'd run into a dead end."

So I went the way the men told me to except the town I went through took me two minutes to drive through. I was through both in five minutes, including driving around the oil plant, which was really only a fenced-in area with a small warehouse and three trucks inside, but it did smell of oil. Then I saw the sign as I was crossing over a creek, a sign made of planks nailed to a 2 x 4 sticking out of the ground saying "Welcome to McVeigh." I could literally see the other end of town from there.

The two lanes had a creek running through on one side, so to get to the homes you had to cross that. There were only about twelve homes on that side, and maybe the same on the other side of the road. No stores or gas stations. The homes were high and low, a few were halfway up the mountain.

I passed one vehicle, and one of us just about went into the ditch because of the road not being wide enough for two. Guess which vehicle was close to going into the ditch? Glad I was driving a Jeep with 4-wheel drive.

By this time, the two-lane road had turned into a lane and a half. As I drove through the rest of the town there were no more homes, and the road leading out of town turned into one lane. At the end of the two-lane there was a curve in the road going out of town so I stopped and saw nothing beyond that; if I wanted to see more, I would have to go beyond that curve.

I still had some light left, although it was three in the afternoon and I knew that it got dark in the mountains early. I thought I had time enough to go a few more miles down the road and return. My better judgment told me not to go around that curve. But sometimes one doesn't listen to one's better judgment, so I moved on.

Part Two

AROUND THE CURVE the road went up but again, since I had a 4-wheel-drive vehicle, I wasn't worried. After about an hour it occurred to me that this was it, this was McVeigh. What happened to the railroad tracks, the coal processing units? The black side of town and white side of town—but there was no town. Surely there was more to McVeigh than this! There were no signs saying anything about what was ahead or anything like that. So after another 30 minutes or more and seeing nothing but more mountains, and steadily moving up, I started looking for a place to turn around. I didn't find that for another 45 minutes. It wasn't really large enough to turn around but I thought it might do. I almost made it until my right rear tire slid off the road and then my right front slid off. As I put the vehicle in 4-wheel drive it got worse; next thing I knew, the whole rear end was off the road.

I got out and surveyed my situation and it didn't look good. I thought about what I would do if I didn't get myself out of this mess and may have to walk out of here, and with the darkness catching up with me.

Then I thought about the winch I had on the front end of the Jeep; maybe I could use that and tie the winch to a tree and get myself back on track. Worth a try, so I did. I put the winch in neutral and pulled the cable to the nearest tree. After hooking onto the tree, I put the winch back in gear got back in the vehicle and proceeded to try and get the hell on track. There was just one thing; the tree I found was a little left of the Jeep, and that's the way it started pulling. It pulled me into where I didn't want it to go—down the mountain backwards.

I stopped and found I was in worse trouble than before; so much for the winch. I guess it would've helped if I knew how to use that damn thing.

By this time, it had started getting dark and a little chilly, so I thought I'd put on my jacket. I wondered whether I should try and hike my way out of there. I was sure dressed for it; had my hiking boots on and jeans, plus a heavy shirt. I checked my supplies that I keep in the vehicle, especially knowing I was coming up this way.

One pocketknife, one blanket of the thermal version, one 25-foot length of rope, one canteen full of water and one flask half-full of brandy. Hat, jacket, and gloves. Cigarette lighter and one pack of beef jerky. All this I kept in a backpack. Oh yeah, and I also had one MP3 player with headphones, about 200 songs on it and 10 audiobooks, so I was good to go.

Maybe, I thought, I should keep my ass right here with the vehicle until the next day; that would be the wise thing to do. I had checked my cell phone a number of times but there was no signal; should have known that. Up here in the mountains it's dark when it's light, if you know what I mean.

I checked out my situation again and saw that alone, there was no way I was getting out of there, so I sat back in the Jeep and took me a hit of the brandy. Put my headphones on and started listening to some of my old tunes, something happy, like Junior Walker and the All-stars' "Road Runner." By this time it had really gotten dark, and it was only 7:00 p.m.

This was gonna be a long night. About 11 P.M that night I saw lights coming my way from above on that same road I was on; looked like torches, about 20 of them. *Help has come at last!* I thought, and as they came closer I strained my eyes and said to myself, "Ghosts?" Whoever was holding the torches were all in white. Then I said, "I don't believe in ghosts," so the only thing I could think of in this part of the woods were Klan, as in Ku Klux Klan. I might be wrong but I wasn't sticking around to find out.

I picked up my backpack and MP3 player and headed up the side of the mountain. After I got so far I stopped and turned around so I could look back down toward where I thought my Jeep was—it was that damn dark. Climbing the side of the mountain wasn't as easy as it looked. I was slipping and sliding most of the way, and sometimes even crawling. But I made it to a spot that I thought was far enough away that was safe. At my age I was breathing rather hard, so I sat down and took a hit of brandy and waited. Fifteen minutes later my ghosts arrived at my vehicle and stopped, looked around, and started discussing something I couldn't hear.

Then they all got together and unhooked the winch from the tree I had put it around and placed it on another tree to give the Jeep a more direct pull, and in 10 minutes they had the vehicle on the road and turned the way I'd come. In my haste to get away from the Jeep I had forgotten my keys in the ignition. They started the Jeep and continued down the road, with the Jeep in the lead. What the hell? I decided to follow; nothing else to do. It wasn't easy. A half-mile down the road they turned off into an area I never noticed on the way up. The turnoff was kind of camouflaged, as far as I could tell, but my Jeep lights lit it up pretty good. Once they were through, I went down and crossed the road to the opening. If I hadn't seen them go through, I would never have known it was there. It was a gate, covered by tree limbs and branches.

I opened it just far enough so I could squeeze through and started following the ghosts and my Jeep. On my way through, I passed a tree that had a rope tied around the trunk and leading up the tree. I didn't want to put my flashlight on for fear of my friends noticing it, but what I did do was shake the rope and as I did, something started swinging up there.

The moon was out somewhat and I could see the silhouette of a person; it was that of a hanging man. I thought about Billie Holiday's old song "Strange Fruit." When I first heard it as a boy it took me a long while before I understood what it meant. Not about fruits at all, but blacks being hung from trees. I shook my head and started to go back and take my chances on the road but I felt I'd come too far. I had to get my Jeep back to have any chance at all of getting out of there in one piece. So I continued following the ghosts. A half-mile down, in a clearing, my ghosts were in a half-circle, still holding their torches. There in the middle of the circle was a cross of about 30 feet in length, and one of the ghosts was putting what I guess was gas on it and lighting it. I was watching all this at the tree line laying on my stomach. I knew right then I wanted no part of this but I had no choice; they had my Jeep.

Speaking of my Jeep, it was on the far side of the clearing. It would take me a while to get there. So I just laid there because right behind where my Jeep was parked, ten more ghosts came out of the woods.

So I just laid there and watched the festivities. Now about thirty ghosts were there all around the cross, which was burning brightly by this time. Everyone's arms went up in a Hitler salute and all were saying, "Heil, Hitler!" I grabbed my flask out of my backpack and took another long hit and continued watching the spectacle.

An hour later, the party started breaking up. My ghosts started disrobing and I got a chance to see who was behind those sheets. There were young men, old men, young women, and old women; all white. Some of the young women looked pretty damn good. Some of the men looked like bankers, others looked like salesman and typical businessmen, farmers, and layman. But then we always knew that it's not behind the sheets so much anymore. Now it's the business suits, the dinner dress, and the teachers holding the kids back.

But here they are now grouped together, all for one and one for themselves. The group started moving out after putting the fire out on the cross. The torches stayed lit and they all started moving out. I was prepared for them to come out the way they came in and I was about to move to another location but they fooled me; they left from behind my Jeep where that last bunch had come in.

I had no idea where they were headed, but there was something back that way, and I didn't want to know. Everyone left the area except two. They got into the Jeep and began driving toward the road and the gate. I took another quick hit from my flask and started toward the gate myself.

Then I heard someone call from the tree line on the other side of the clearing. One of the guys in the Jeep acknowledge the person who had called. After stopping the Jeep, he drove back and got out and started conferring with the person back there. I started running toward the gate; didn't know what I intended to do when I got there, but this is what I knew; this would be the last chance for me to get my Jeep back and I was not going to pass it up.

By the time I was near the gate, the Jeep's headlights hit me in the ass. I moved over to the tree line and searched around for a weapon, eventually finding a tree branch about three feet long and very solid. When the Jeep got to the gate and stopped, it had only one man in it, not two, and he hadn't seen me; my luck was beginning to change.

The person got out to open the gate. When he returned and was entering the vehicle, I came up behind him and laid the tree limb to the back of his head. He fell out like a log. I pulled him away from the Jeep and laid him on the side of the road, threw my backpack in the back of the Jeep, got in and drove away. I proceeded down the hill through McVeigh and the other two towns to the main highway and headed for Texas. Two hundred miles down the road I stopped for gas and to pee. I finished the rest of my brandy, and didn't stop again for another 300 miles. Only then did I feel safe and could breathe freely again.

Well, so much for wanting to see my birthplace. I came, I saw, and now I'm out of there!

Epilogue

BACK HOME IN my apartment, I thought about that trip and how it could have turned out entirely different. They could have found me out there in the woods. I could have ended up like the person hanging from the tree. What if I had waited there at the Jeep expecting help? Look who would have shown up. What if it was me laying out by the gate instead of one of the ghosts? I thought about reporting the hanging person to the authorities, but I didn't know who was who in that group of ghosts; one could even be a law enforcement officer. Hey, it's happened before.

So I kept driving out of Kentucky, through Tennessee, and back home to Texas. I wasn't born here but it's my home now. I picked up my glass of brandy, laid my head back on my La-Z-Boy, and waited for the old girl to call.

Chicago after Dark

Part One

JANUARY 2010, Chicago, Illinois. I was walking down the Magic Mile, dressed in a crew cap, an overcoat that reached my ankles, two sweaters, shirt, and T-shirt. Insulated pants, thermal socks, and Alaskan-style boots, and I was still cold. I had just left the clothing store and they assured me that the clothing I had purchased would keep me warm. They lied.

I'd left Hawaii a week ago, where it was a nice 87° to come here, to Chicago, where it was a very cold 37°. How the hell did I ever get here? Let me take it back a pace.

A week earlier I was laying on the beach at Waikiki under an umbrella, a cooler by my side filled with various drinks. Couple bottles of beer, fifth of vodka with tonic already mixed, and a bottle of wine for the lady. Oh yeah, a fine Indonesian beauty of 22 was beside me. Five foot two, hundred twenty pounds, long, black hair to her waist. Bikini—almost! Halter untied and laying on her stomach. I was putting lotion on her back. I had just finished putting it on her behind, and what a nice behind she had. Nola and I had been laying up together for close to a week while she was on vacation and this was her last day in Hawaii, she would be going home the next day. We planned on making the most of this last day/night.

I live in Hawaii, and had been for the last six months. I moved here right after I was released from prison, with a few stops in between. My friend Centrale kind of helped me out there.

Centrale is an alien I met before going to jail and he helped me out while I was there. While I was in the hole he got me things like books, let me watch TV, and sent me dinners that I wouldn't ordinarily get in there. Steak, lobster, and Taco Bell. He also arranged for me to get out for a time from midnight to six in the morning. I met up with my girlfriend and basically just lived it up; I didn't want to leave. I found out that Centrale could do lots of things, and for all the three years I was incarcerated, he did. He just wouldn't break me out of jail permanently. He did ask for favors that he couldn't do himself, but that's another story.

I put Nola on her flight the next day and we made arrangements to meet same time next year. I returned to the beach and laid under that same umbrella and thought about the past week and started missing Nola already.

"Hello, John? Are you there, John?"

I knew it was too good to last. Centrale, my alien friend, hadn't contacted me in a while now and I was hoping… maybe! Centrale contacted me telepathically, he just pops up in my mind. Crazy, I know, but there he is. Centrale is outside the earth's atmosphere on a spacecraft.

"Centrale, haven't heard from you in a while, how you been?"

"I'm fine John, I hope you are rested up."

"That don't sound good, Centrale, what's up?"

"I'm glad you're so enthusiastic about it. We have a problem in Chicago, Illinois, that we think you may be able to help us with."

"Chicago? You do realize this is January. I's cold as hell in Chicago right now. It must be at least 20° or 30°. You don't have anything in say, Jamaica or the Bahamas, someplace like that?"

"Afraid not, John. Wear warm clothes."

"Okay, Centrale, what you got?"

"The person we had in Chicago died. He was another like you."

"For some reason I thought your people didn't die; and here I was, thinking I'd be living forever."

"No, John, don't think that way. You still die just like everybody else."

"And what about you, Centrale? Do you die? By the way, how old are you, anyway?"

"I am 150 years by human count, and yes, we also die, eventually."

"Okay, okay, so when do I leave?"

"You have a week, John, so enjoy the beach while you can."

"You want to tell me why you're sending me to cold-ass Chicago?"

"Yes, John, to make a wrong right again."

Part Two

"THE CITY OF Chicago is out of control. The gangs are going rabid and killing whoever, and there is no law to speak of. When there is, they're killing more people than the gangs. The entire system is corrupt! Your job, John, is to even out the playing field."

"Centrale, couldn't you have done this at another time, say summertime?

It happens when it happens, John. Keep me informed of your progress.

Any idea where I should start?

Start at the bottom, John, and work up. There is enough killing going on that it shouldn't take long for you to tone in on the ones who are perpetrating all this.

The Hamilton Hotel; not the best, but for what my needs were, this would do. I appeared in front of the counter and the clerk looked up in surprise and said, "How did you get in here? The door was locked."

You must be mistaken, I said. It was unlocked. How else would I get in?

Yeah, I guess you're right. In this neighborhood we have to lock the doors, sorry. What can I do for you?

I'll need a single for a few days, maybe even longer, I'll let you know.

In my room I noticed it really wasn't that bad; I've been in worse. I didn't enter the hotel through the door because I didn't have to. I really didn't know if it was locked or not because I was transported there. One of the powers Centrale has is he can transport a person from one spot to another. He was doing it himself, but after he saw he could trust me, he gave that power to me, along with other powers.

I thought I'd turn the TV on and catch all the news, but first I called the counter to see if I could get a bottle sent up. I know this place is not so cheap that they can't do that. I guess I could use my transport powers but I don't want to overdo it. Thirty minutes later my fifth of vodka arrived and I settled back and began watching the local news.

Breaking news: a group of men used a stolen truck to break into a convenience store. They made a big mess but left empty-handed. Two men were caught beating up on a homeless man, both were taken to jail and the homeless man to the hospital. A hit-and-run driver was caught on camera in a pickup truck hitting a teenager. They're looking for that driver. Another police officer shot and killed another teenager while he was running away. The officer said he was in fear for his life. The teenager was shot 12 times in the back, mostly while he was on the ground.

Drive-by shootings claimed the lives of three; one 16, one 12, and one 18-month-old baby girl. All were sitting on their porch listening to music. Leaving the scene was a red 2008 Ford pickup truck with wire wheels with two black occupants, one wearing a mask, the other with dreadlocks. A Glock was pointing out the window. The shooting is under investigation.

Two police detectives and four officers have been cleared by the grand jury. The case they were indicted for was holding four civilians against their will for four weeks without being charged. This is the third case of officers being charged with officer oppression and them being released. This is the third time protesters have had protest marches in front of the courthouse; no one expects anything will be done this time, either.

I cut off the TV; that's enough of that bullshit. Centrale was right, Chicago is a mess. I don't know what the hell I can do, but whatever it is, I'm sure people will get hurt, and probably not the ones expected. I poured myself another drink and called down to the desk to see if they could send me something up to my room to eat. The counter person told me he was sorry but his runner had just been in an accident and wouldn't be back for another hour or more. "There is a Mexican restaurant about two blocks away if you don't mind fighting the snow." I thanked the clerk looked in the phone book and found the address and transported myself right there.

The waitress came over to the table and said, "I'm sorry, sir, I didn't notice you sitting here. Have you been waiting long?

"No, not long at all. I think I'll order the burrito dinner. And what about a vodka on the rocks?"

***

I had brought my coat with me, even though I didn't have to, but I figured I had to get out there sometime so why not now. I'd start by walking back to the motel, two blocks away; I could do that. The street still had snow on it but you could still drive up the middle, the snowplow at least kept that clean. Someone had been cleaning the sidewalks but I did slip a few times from some ice still being there. Chicago means the wind was a killer, and it was that night.

I made it to the corner and only fell down twice. I stayed close to the buildings, trying to cut down on the wind. No one was on the streets during this time of the year; I can see why.

I could now see my motel at the other end of the block so I tried picking up speed. Between myself and my motel, a teenager shot out of the alley and into the middle of the street. He was shot in the back by someone I couldn't see until they came into view. A police officer came running out with a gun held in both hands and started firing again as the teenager laid there.

Without thinking, I used one of the powers Centrale had given me and plugged up his weapon during his firing. The weapon blew up and took his hands off. He dropped to his knees and started screaming.

I walked over to where the kid was laying and checked for a pulse but before I did, I knew he was dead. I looked over at the cop, who was still screaming about his hands and holding them in front of him (or what was left of them) and saying, "Help me, help me!" I stood there and looked at him for about five seconds and continued on my way to the motel. The officer screamed at me to help him. "Fuck you," I said.

I got to the motel door and the clerk opened up. "Did you hear that gunfire down the street a few minutes ago? Did you see anything?"

"Not me, didn't see or hear a thing."

The next morning before breakfast, I turned on the early morning news and sat back with a cup of coffee. ABC Chicago 14 reported that: "Late last night, a police officer was attacked after trying to apprehend a criminal. He managed to shoot the man but his accomplish shot the gun out of the officer's hand and in turn the weapon exploded. There was a witness to the action but he didn't stick around to call for help. The officer managed to call in by the radio on his vest. The police are searching for that witness."

They said nothing about the teenager shot in the back; guess he didn't matter.

Where do I start? I need to let them know I'm here; how do I go about that? I think maybe at the City Council, I'll start there.

Ten o'clock that morning, the City Council was having their weekly meeting with the mayor in charge. The person at the podium was a lady about 68 years old, telling them there was little to no police presence in her neighborhood. "We hardly ever see them unless they're killing or beating up somebody. This has got to stop!"

The mayor told her that her concerns would be looked into. "Next!"

"That was the last speaker, Mr. Mayor," one of the councilmembers said. Just before he dropped his gavel to close the meeting for the week, I appeared at the podium.

"Where did you come from?" the mayor asked. "I thought we were finished here."

I thought so too one of the other members said. The people in the auditorium were in awe because only a few saw me just appear out of nowhere.

You want to tell us, sir, who you are? And can it wait until our next meeting?

No, sir, it can't, and you will want to hear what I have to say.

The members of the council were half out their seats, but found they couldn't move any father. The mayor said, Sorry, you will have to come back next week. But when he tried to move, he couldn't. All eight were stuck right where they were; those who were half-standing, I allowed to sit.

"What the hell is this?" the mayor said. "Why can't we move? You some kind of a Martian or something? Whatever you're doing, I need you to stop."

The people in the audience were all awake and giving it their full attention and all saying under their breath, who the hell is this guy?"

My name is John Chandler, and I was sent here by an alien in the outer atmosphere. I'm here to correct what's wrong with the city of Chicago. Your police are out of control. You, the monitors of the police, are doing nothing, and don't seem to think anything about the people. The gangs are running rampant, the elderly can't walk the streets for fear of being intimidated, and children can't play in the playground for fear of being shot. Nothing is being done to change, that's why I'm here. I'm here to change things, and I'm here to replace you if necessary.

The people in the audience started clapping their hands, hollering: "Yeah, man, that's what's needed!" The older people were saying: "Thank the Lord!" There was one newsman in the chamber where there's normally none, and he started taking pictures and videos. "Who the hell are you?" the mayor said, "to come in here and threaten this council. Do you even live here in Chicago? Sergeant at arms, get this man the hell out of here!

As the sergeant started moving toward me, I put up my hand and the sergeant stopped in his tracks. "In the coming week you will understand the power of Centrale. You will either comply or feel his anger. You will no longer be allowed to continue the abuse to your people that you have. Stay tuned."

With that, I disappeared. The council and sergeant at arms were able to move but no one left the meeting.

The mayor was the first to speak. what the hell was that all about, will someone tell me?

Three days later there was a meeting of the top gang members of Chicago, put together by the local pastors, imploring them for peace and to think of the people in the neighborhood; the kids in the hood, the collateral damage they were doing. "Please stop! One group accuses the other, one accuses the police, and another the economics." The meeting was held in one of the largest churches in the city. There were four groups, all in their own colors. One group had on a majority of red, one was in blue, one in green and black, another all in black and yellow. All were sitting in their own sections. Two hundred gang members were present in all. There were four pastors with one on the podium, trying to hold it all together.

I showed up standing right beside the pastor at the lectern. "May I say a word, Pastor?"

The pastor started to ask something, but I put up my hand to stop. The other pastors all stood up behind him, and many of the gang members did the same.

"My name is John Chandler. A few days ago, I spoke at your City Council. You may have heard about it. Basically, I'm going to tell you the same thing I told them. The drive-by shootings, gang fighting, intimidation . . . that has to stop. That will stop. I will not plead with you like these good pastors are trying to do, but I'll tell you what will happen if you don't stop what you're doing. Since I know you won't believe me, I'll have to show you."

What the hell are you talking about? one GM said. Just who the fuck are you to tell us what we can or can't do? Fuck you!

Another jumped up and said, If these good pastors can't tell us shit, how do you think you can? And besides, if one of those punks hits us, we gonna hit back.

Who you calling punks? another said. I'll put a bullet up your ass right here.

I addressed the individual and said, "Go ahead."

They all looked at me and I said, "But if you do that you will have to call a medic, because the hand that holds a weapon will be blown off. What I'm talking about is this; since you won't stop doing what you're doing, then I have taken it upon myself to neutralize your weapons. I could just not let them function, but I believe you won't get the message if I did that. So I decided to take it up a notch, which is to have your weapons explode.

"You jive MF, I don't believe you can do anything like that," a gang member said. "I should blow yo ass away right now, right here." He pulled out a Glock and pointed it at me. "Just say I won't!"

"You won't," I said. The person that held the Glock didn't fire, he just held the weapon pointed at me.

But then one of them dressed in yellow and black ran from the back of the group with a .38 revolver in his hand and said, "I don't know what's wrong with you guys. I'll fuck him up myself!" Then he pulled the trigger. That's when his hand blew off to the wrist. And then there was his screaming and begging for a medic. These were hardened gangbangers and only a few tried to help him. A few even called him a punk, and they were the ones in his own group. The only ones who really tried to help him were the pastors, rushing down and wrapping his injuries. Someone had called for a medic and took him outside to wait. The commotion was tremendous; you could hear it outside the church. Everyone, including the pastors, couldn't believe what just happened.

After the noise died down I said, I know some of you think that was just an accident, just a fluke. But I assure you, it wasn't. Now that I have your attention, let me tell you what will happen in the future; the same thing that just happened to that young man. The same thing that will happen to you each time you do a drive-by. Each time you randomly rob someone and there is a gun involved and is fired. How many hands you lose depends on how you hold your weapon; if you hold it with one hand, then you lose that hand. If you use two hands, let's say you're firing a rifle, then you lose both hands. The elderly and children, they should be able to walk around without being harassed by you. There are other things I'm prepared to do but I think that'll do for now. I hope you do get my meaning. There'll be a few of you who will try me. All I can say is, keep your emergency hospital number on speed dial.

There is just one other thing I want you to know. I'm giving you a heads-up about the drive-bys. I know when you do this there are others in the vehicle with you. If I have to come back, whoever's in the vehicle with the one that pulls the trigger, the same thing will happen to them. Gentlemen, don't make me have to come back."

And then I was gone, just like I appeared.

The commotion started up again, even between the pastors. If it wasn't for the blood on the floor and the sirens of the ambulance outside they would not have believed it, except in the very back of the room was a gang member name Git-U with his cell phone, recording everything that was said and what went down.

Two days later at 2:00 p.m., I was having dinner at a local barbecue restaurant. I'd heard that Chicago had some of the best barbecue in the country. They had the TV on with my picture on it. They were telling of the church and the gang member with his hand blown off and interviews with the pastor and some gang members. They also told of the city council and what happened there; it had all gone viral.

They had me showing up at the council meeting asking, was it just an illusion? The gang members at the church saw it; the blood and their member's hand blown off were real.

After I ate, I paid the bill and was about to leave. The waitress said, "I know you, you were just on TV!"

That same afternoon, two men walked into a convenience store with weapons in hand and commenced to rob the place. After the convenience store owner gave the men the money, one attempted to shoot him. The gun exploded in his hand, taking it off. After the screams, he asked his accomplice to help him. Meanwhile, the clerk was grabbing for his gun. The accomplice ran out of the store, dropping his gun while the clerk was firing after him. The clerk turned his attention toward the other would-be robber. He started to fire, then looked at him on the floor moaning and groaning, pleading for an ambulance. Blood was all over the counter, and some was even on the clerk. He felt sorry for the robber and called the police and ambulance—but not for 10 minutes, after watching him suffer. That very night, the homeboys were driving around looking for revenge on a rival group that had disrespected one of their women. They found a bunch of teens hanging together near a park. They had no idea who they were looking for, but they felt anyone would do because they were sending a message.

One of the boys in the car was Git-U, the same gang member who had the cell phone in the church and took the pictures. He reminded them what happened in the church and advised them that they should give it time to see if this guy was for real. After all, he said, people just don't appear and disappear right in front of your eyes. And don't forget Little Bit, sitting up there in the hospital—with one hand. The shooter told Git-U, "You believe that shit, man? All that was just some bullshit to get your goat. Those guys there on the corner will do just fine."

***

St. Jade hospital emergency room that same night, 11:45 p.m. "This is the third person that's come in here with his hand blown off. If this keeps up, this is going to be a long night, one of the nurses said.

When Git-U and the shooter came in he had his phone out, filming the whole thing. The shooter, through moans, told him, "If you don't put that goddamn phone down I'm going to stick it up your ass." But there in the room were many reporters, as well as average citizens, and they were Tweeting, FaceBooking, Instagramming, and YouTube-ing. Sometimes regular people got the information before the reporters.

Part Three

A WEEK LATER, the police were having their Policeman's Ball. Everyone was there; the governor, the mayor, the chief of police, and every prominent person in the city. The governor was first and he had just finished when the mayor was walking up; that's when I appeared.

The auditorium was ablaze with conversation. The mayor said, You again? We appreciate what you've done for the city. Crime is down 50 percent, and we expect it to go down even more with your help. Mayor, I don't think you'll be thanking me after tonight when I finish telling you what I'm going to tell you.

Then I faced the audience. You are the law enforcement for this entire city, the eyes and ears, the protection. Yet you don't protect all; you pick and choose the ones you protect, and they're mostly the wealthy. This is not something I've dreamed up, but something I know from the top, your mayor, to the bottom, the officer on the beat. I'm not saying the majority of you are corrupt, but a good many are. The others, since you remain silent, I'll have to include you along with the rest. There are killers among you; I know it, and you know it, but still you remain silent. I'm here to correct that injustice. I'm here to tell you—no, to *demand* you change your ways.

An officer jumped up in the audience and said, "Or what? What can you do? Here in Chicago we're 20,000 strong; we are the law."

I raised my hand and the officer came out of his seat and kept on rising until he reached the ceiling 50 feet above. I kept him up there for a good 15 seconds to let everyone know that it wasn't a fluke, and then let him drop back down to his seat. The fall broke both his legs, and the two people alongside of him were injured.

I returned to what I was saying. I've spoken to the City Council. I've also spoken to the gangs of the city and made them aware of what's coming down the road. Now I'm telling you. The harassments, disrespect, beatings, and humiliations, all must stop. The shootings in the back multiple times. All those things you will no longer be allowed to do. The Tasing two and three times; that's unnecessary. After the first time, if it's not necessary, the volt will return to you. The blue line… If you want to live by the line, then you shell die by the line. Governor and Mayor, if you don't rein in your people, the hammer will come down on you.

By this time the auditorium was in chaos and everyone was arguing with each other, hollering at me, and a few of the officers started fighting. The media was in the back taking it all in. I felt then was a good time to leave, and I did.

Part Four

In my hotel room I picked up the bottle of vodka, a glass of ice, and sat on the couch. Now all I had to do was wait; wait and see what would go down. I didn't think they'd listen to me the first time around; if not, I'd have to up the ante.

Days later, Officer Struthers and his partner, Officer Jensen, were on patrol in their squad car. Halfway down the block they noticed a black man with no coat, running down the sidewalk. They decided to stop him because he looked suspicious. Just one problem; he wouldn't stop.

Officer Struthers thought he'd get out and chase him. Officer Jensen said he'd drive ahead of him and stop him on the corner. Officer Struthers slipped on a patch of ice while chasing the suspect, cracking his ankle, and had to stop his pursuit. Jensen had stopped down the block and got out of his vehicle, waiting on the suspect. He was moving pretty fast, even with the ice and snow on the ground, but he did manage to blow past Officer Jensen before he had a chance to grab him.

As he passed, Officer Jensen fired at him with his stun gun, hitting him in the back and taking him down. Up to that point, it seemed like a righteous takedown.

But he still had no idea what the man had done. No probable cause other than the guy was running. He walked over to him, took the darts out of his back and kicked him in the side. "That's for running and fucking up my day."

Jensen began getting out his cuffs when the suspect started groaning from being Tased and said, "Please don't Tase me again, Officer!"

You don't decide how many times you get Tased, I do. And since you asked, here is another one, and he stood over him and fired. The volts that were supposed to go into the suspect reversed and came right back into the officer instead, twice the amount. Officer Jensen stood in the middle of the street shaking worse than the suspect had. The suspect had revived himself by this time, looked at the officer holding his stun gun, and shook his head and continued on his way. The tapes on the squad car told the tale of Jensen Tasing the suspect and about to Tase him again while he was on the ground, and just as I had said the volts would do, they returned to the officer. Officer Jensen was still in the hospital a week later.

The torture house....

One other stop I felt I had to make was the torture house, what the victims call the house of pain.

Part Five

Detectives Glenn and So Lo were interrogating a young woman of
about 22. She was known to be the girlfriend of the Latin Kings gang
leader. Five people had been murdered in the last three weeks, but
none by gunfire; all by strangulation or knife. The girlfriend was
believed to hold the secret to who, where, and when.

When the detectives started their interrogation, it didn't matter to them if it was a man or woman; they had been interrogating her for over eight hours and felt they were making progress. Regardless of that, Detective So So would slap her upside the head when it looked like she was nodding off. She had been held for three days with no charges against her, nothing to eat and little to drink. She was sitting in a straight-back chair held only by shackles to her ankles and those to the floor, connected to a ring. She had heard others being interrogated, some even tortured. She was told they were taking her to police headquarters when she was first picked up but she ended up there, in the house of pain.

The first thing she did was ask for a lawyer, but all they did was laugh at her. She stayed almost two days in their basement before being taken upstairs and being questioned, if you want to call it that. She lasted as long as she could and then she began talking. They knew she would; they always do. Detective Glenn had been an interrogator in Vietnam and was very good at his job; one hundred percent success so far.

There were two other houses in different parts of the city, three in all. One was found out and closed, but the other two were still working.

With the girl spilling the beans, they should be able to close this case in no time. She also told them that in the place they were located they had many weapons, and that was right up So Lo and Glenn's alley.

At 2:00 a.m., Glenn and So Lo were washing their hands and patting each other on the back on a job well done while the girl watched. She knew if the Latin Kings found out that she had informed on them, she was dead meat. They didn't care if she had been tortured or not.

As Glenn was washing his hands, he glanced in the mirror and saw this black man sitting on the couch with his legs crossed. "What the fuck? How the hell did you get in here and who the hell are you?"

So Lo said, Glenn, you don't recognize this dude? That's the guy from the council meeting, the Policeman's Ball, and that church with the gangbangers. I think he be bad news.

I don't give a rat's ass who he is, he needs to get the fuck out of here.

I've been telling you for years, Glenn, you need to keep up with current events.

Your partner's telling you right, Glenn, you should listen to him.

I'm not listening to shit. I'm about to put a foot up your ass if you don't get the hell out of here.

Detective So Lo, I feel I can talk to you. How many more hostages do you have in this building?

Don't tell him shit, So So. Fuck him.

We got four, including the girl, So Lo said.

First thing I want you to do, Detective, is release them. You can start with the girl here.

Like hell! Glenn said, and pulled his police revolver out and pointed it at me.

Glenn, So Lo said, Don't pull that trigger or the weapon will explode and you'll be short two hands.

Detective Glenn hesitated a minute and thought of the stories he'd been hearing around town about this guy and decided not to fire. *Goddamn,* he thought, *I can't shoot him, I can't Tase him; what the hell can I do to him?*

While he was thinking it out, I pointed at the girl's shackles and they unlocked. I told her to go.

Go my ass, Glenn said, and ran at me. But before he got to me I had raised my hand. Glenn stopped in his tracks as though he had run into a brick wall and he was out like a light.

The girl had gotten up and was headed out the door. I said to her, "You were never here."

Detective So Lo just stood where he was, not knowing what to do, not even attending to his partner. "Detective So Lo, here's what I want you to do. Release the rest of your hostages, and the remaining officers, I want them to get out. Contact your other building and tell them to cease operation. Can you remember all that, Detective?"

Detective So Lo did what he was told, starting with taking Detective Glenn out of the house. The other officers wanted to know what was going on; So Lo told them about John Chandler.

One officer asked about all the evidence they had acquired. "What do we do about that?"

"Leave it," I said.

Once I verified that everyone was out of the house, I started lighting the place up.

Part Six

THE MAYOR, chief of police, and city manager were speaking about me at a noon luncheon. The mayor was saying, "But it's working. Whatever the hell he's doing is working. The drive-bys are down or nonexistent. We had a number of hands blown off, so we can equate that with drive-bys that turned sour on the shooters. People are starting to walk the streets and parks at night without fear of someone taking them out. The robberies are down; none being carried out with a gun, anyway; maybe a stick or a knife. And don't forget, the clerks in the stores can still use their weapons for protection.

All that's good, Mayor, said the chief, but a few of my men have also lost hands. What about that?

If you investigate, Chief, I have a feeling you'll find out they were in the wrong. Since we're on that subject, Chief, I hear two of your houses were burned down and your men stood around and did nothing.

Well, Mayor, what would you have us do? We can't shoot or Tase the guy. If we try and take him out any other way, we're fucked. If you have any suggestions, I'm open for it.

Does anyone know where John's holing up? Where he's staying?

Yes, we do, Mayor, but we didn't want to make a move on him, and even if we did, what could we do? The people like him and what he's doing.

Chief, we have to do something. He's taken over the town and we're losing more and more officers.

More training, that's what we need is more training, said the city manager. But I'll have to tell you, we just have some stupid officers. They'll do shit knowing they have video cameras on them all the while and they do it anyway. Stupid!

Back to John, the mayor said. Should we try picking him up?

I'm against it, the chief said. We know what the man is capable of. If we tried what you suggest all hell would break loose, and don't forget, someone will have to take the fall if things don't go right. Who's it gonna be, Mayor?

Everyone in the city was getting kind of comfortable, even the gangs. Now they didn't have to worry about drive-bys, only when running and protecting their drugs. But using 13- and 14-year-olds, no one ever catches them.

Yeah, things were going pretty smooth. That damn Git U got over like a fat rat. Some movie people picked him up and hired him and were making a documentary of all those videos he'd been taking. They headed off to Hollywood; I guess that'll be the last time we ever see him.

The pastors were very happy. They hadn't had a funeral in weeks now, thanks to me. And they also noticed a few of the gang members coming to Sunday morning services.

Maybe it's happening, one of the pastor's said. They're finally becoming civilized again.

One of the parishioners told the pastors that she didn't know how to act. "My husband and I went for a stroll on River Drive walkway."

That was nice, the pastor said. But what was so unusual about that?

At 10:45 at night, she said.

Say no more, the pastor said.

John! Are you there, John?

I'm here, Centrale. sorry I haven't contacted you, but I've been kind of busy. I went on to tell Centrale everything I'd done since I've been here.

Centrale listened to it all and eventually said, You did a good job, John, and we couldn't have asked any more of you. We never expected you to do as good as you did. This was an experiment; we never planned for it to last, but just to show what it could be like. Some things we could have done better, but, all in all you did good, John. I have good news for you; we're about to pull you out. Is there anything else you want to do before you leave?

I've been wanting to hear those words, Centrale, but you know, I think the place is starting to grow on me. Wind, snow, cold, ice, and all. Is there anything else I haven't accomplished? I can't think of any. Everything's in place. They have a year to conform; after that, they're on their own. I wish them well.

That night at nine, I was back at the Mexican restaurant ordering from that same waitress. "You know, I get off at ten, she said. What about coming over to my place?"

"You know, that's what I like about you people in Chicago. You don't bite your tongue about anything."

"Life is too short for that. What about it?"

"Count me in."

I left the waitress's apartment at around eight the next morning, transported myself to my hotel and put on the coffee, took a shower and changed my clothes. Well, I thought, *another job well done. In another hour or so I'm out of here.*

The phone rang and I answered it. The clerk said, Mr. Chandler, there are some policemen headed up to your room, thought you'd want to know.

There was a knock at the door and I opened it up. The mayor, chief of police, city manager, and two members of the SWAT team stood there. They didn't ask whether or not they could come in but just walked past me and into the room.

Mr. Chandler, the mayor said, We're here to arrest you for disturbing the peace of the city, for blowing the hands off many police officers, burning down at least two homes, intervening in police business, and anything else we can think of.

Mayor, do you really think you can arrest me? You know what I can do.

Yes, we know, Mr. Chandler, but we have to try. Society has to know who is in control and that would be us, the law.

All that would be good, Mayor, if you only acted like the law. That's why I'm here. What is your proposition?

We will drop all charges if you'll just leave town. Number two, drop all the blocks you have against the police. Number three, you can leave all blocks against the gangs and others.

So basically leave everything the way it was before I came, that right?

Yeah, that's about it, said the chief.

It'll never happen, I said. The only thing I will do is depart the city of Chicago. The rules I put into place will stay, for the next year at least.

And if we don't go along with you and arrest you anyway?

How many men do you have here with you, Mr. Mayor; 20, 30? There'll be at least that many losing their hands—and you as leader of the city would also lose yours. Are you prepared for that, Mr. Mayor? I've got to go take a leak, you all talk about it; take your time.

Jamaica, a week later…

Now this is where it's at; 82° at the beach, women in bikinis looking more beautiful than ever, a cooler full of beer, and no problems. This is the life.

Chicago during the day was really something else. But Chicago after dark…

Beauty on a stick

Part 1

WHAT IS IT ABOUT a fine woman. She's fine until six months into her, then it's like she stops been fine anymore. Everyone who sees her tells you she's fine and says, "How in the hell did you get a fine thing like that?"

And you say, "Oh, that's just Etta, my girlfriend." What is it that makes a man do that? 'Bout the same with an automobile you been wanting. After you get it, six months later it's just another automobile. What is that!? Right after you get it you looking at something else. Same with a woman. Regardless of how nice she is, you looking across the street. Thing is, while you looking that way, somebody else is looking toward you and that's a fact, never fails. Look at all the movie stars. They find bitches everywhere. They don't know which way to turn, that's why they marry so many times. Too many find bitches.

It's not only the men, women do the same damn thing. Hollywood is full of fine men too, and the women act like they can't control themselves. Damn whoremongers!

I remember getting into an argument with a woman about Elizabeth Taylor marrying so many times; eight, I believe. She says she did that because she loved those men, but call it like it is, pure lust. Just like us men want everything we see, so do they. Can't keep it in our pants; if they are offering, we are taking. A person falls in love but once, the rest is outright lust. If women were fine and that's it, like the bar, you reach it and that's it, that's fine, you've reached the top, but it doesn't work like that. Once you reach the top there is a woman finer than the one you have, and that's the way it goes. On and on and on to infinity. Age will catch you before they run out of fine women and then you're too old to enjoy them. But the damnedest thing is your mind is still saying, *I want this,* but your body no longer wants to follow through.

Then there is the time when you get older and the women start to lose their flair; the bikinis, the split skirts and the near nakedness no longer does it for you. What do you do but move on; but move on to what? You no longer drink so that's out. All you can do now is go for walks in the park and feed the pigeons or go to the library. Or then you may reminisce about all the fine young ladies you encountered in your life. Sad!

There is always one that stands out over and above the others, the Queen Bee, you might say. The one that gets all the attention. She's fine and she knows it; everyone else knows it. There are girls who are fine and it never fazes them, then there are girls that use it to the hilt, beyond the bar. I knew a girl like that once. She was one in a million and I'll never forget her.

I met Janet in 1955; well, I didn't know her personally, but knew of her. We were in the same school. She was 16 at the time and I was 17 and just about to graduate. Janet was right behind me. Five foot two, 115 pounds, short bob haircut, an athletic build, like one that would play volleyball and tennis. Every guy in school wanted to date her, including me, but my dollars wasn't long enough for her so I just stood around like the others whose bread wasn't large enough either, all with our tongues hanging out and wishing.

Naturally, she dated the quarterback of our football team and eventually had him going around in circles until he couldn't concentrate and lost his QB position. Then there was the mayor's son, with his convertible and flashy clothes. He hung in there with her for about a month until she dropped him. That is, after he had bought her all those flashy clothes, too. He would have given her his car if his parents hadn't stepped in.

Peter Morris was one of those quiet guys, and somehow she got her hooks into him, I mean really got her hooks into him. He was like a lapdog to her; every place she went he was there waiting for her. In the morning on the school steps, outside her classes after they were over, driving her home after school, buying her lunches, etc., he had it bad. He lasted longer than most. But the thing about Peter was, he still hung around after she cut him loose. Even after she started seeing someone else. She tried talking to him and telling him that it was over and he told her it would never be over, never. Her current boyfriend got tired of him dogging them wherever they went so he got a couple of his friends and put a beating on Peter that Janet concurred with. *Maybe that'll stop him,* she thought. It didn't.

By this time, word had gotten around school and he was the center of many jokes. All he could say was, "What would you do if you loved someone?"

The principal got wind of what was going on and called them both into his office. Sat them both down next to each other. Janet explained that they were together at one time but now she had moved on and hoped he would also.

That sounds fair, Peter, the principal said. Why don't you want to move on just like Janet?

I love her! Peter said.

That's not the way life works, the principal said. You can't force your affections on someone who rejects them. Do you understand, Peter?

Peter said, I was hoping she'd change her mind. He looked at her, tears in his eyes, saying, "Won't you change your mind, please?

Janet just shook her head, not saying anything, but no, she wouldn't change her mind.

Okay, that's it then. I don't want to hear any more about Janet and Peter. Is that clear? the principal said.

I went on to graduate and join the military; two years in Korea and another in Germany, so I didn't hear anything about what went on in my hometown. When I did, it was through Facebook. It seemed like Peter never stopped following Janet. He was arrested numerous times. It had gotten so bad that Janet's parents moved her out of town to live with her aunt. Janet fell right back into her same old bag, leading fellows on, stringing them on for everything they had. But the word I got was that with all those relationships she had, Janet was still a virgin. That accounts for her not being with one guy too long. It doesn't matter how fine a girl was then, she had to give out sooner or later, more sooner than later. Or the guys are moving on, fine or not.

But of course, they told everyone they had scored; you know how it is. It's an image thing. Janet and the boy were in the backseat, he on top of her, trying to get her panties down and she was saying, "Wait, we have to wait a while, Harvey, it's too soon."

Harvey's saying, "Wait? I've waited now for over a month. I think now is the time; you played me long enough."

Janet was about to answer him when she noticed a shadow at the window and screamed. Harvey turned around to see for himself and when he did, his face was blown off by a sawed-off shotgun. All his brains and gore covered Janet and she went berserk. The figure at the window, just before he shot her, paused to give her a good look at him so there would be no doubt of who was pulling the trigger. It was Peter.

.

To whom it may concern

I, BENJAMIN HECKER, did on 17 June 2010 kill Matthew Bartholomew at the Rankin Hotel in Denver, Colorado, room number 1514, by throwing him out the window. I could say it was an accident but that would be a lie. I intended tossing him out of the 15th floor window during a fight. I also killed Emma (my wife) by strangling her. She and Matthew were having an affair. As always, the husband is the last to know.

Matthew and I had been friends for over 10 years. He was my best man at my wedding. He would also look after Emma when I went on my business trips. Now that I think about it, what a laugh. How long it had been going on I have no idea, but I'm thinking for a very long time. The signs were there, they always were; I just didn't pick up on them. I'd leave on my trips for sometimes a week at a time. Emma and I would keep in touch by cell phone, even by Skype, but we'd seldom miss a day. Sometimes when we talked by Skype and we could see each other I could have sworn I saw someone was there with her but most times I'd had a few too many drinks and just passed it off. Other times she'd say, "Have you been drinking again? I believe you've had too many, go to bed."

My job was that of a salesman for a petrochemical company, and sometimes I traveled all over the world. A few times I took Emma. She loved it; or, I thought she did anyway. I would have taken her more often but she'd say she had work to do and couldn't go, or her mother was coming to visit, or something like that. All bullshit, I found out later. She and my friend Matthew were living it up, and a lot was on my dime.

Matthew had never kept a job for all the years I'd known him. I don't know why we stayed friends so long. There are people you just like, regardless of their faults. I knew Matthew was a player, but knew he would never play on me, never go after my woman, we were too close. So I thought.

And her . . . why would she do something like that to me? I'd given her everything she ever wanted. Big house, three cars, fancy clothes, and vacations all over the world; still, that wasn't enough for her. What does it take?

My job is a salesman, like I said earlier, but that's just on paper. My real job is that of an assassin. I assassinate people for various other people, all with the company's blessings. I've been at this now since before I got married.

I've made hits while my wife was with me; she even helped, whether she knew it or not. Once we were in Paris and taking an underground train and I was supposed to off this person. The platform was very crowded. I hadn't planned to hit him there but I thought, why look a gift horse in the mouth? I maneuvered Emma up close to him and when the train came I just bumped up into him and he fell off the platform and onto the tracks. The train couldn't stop in time; another unfortunate accident. Emma was shaken up some but she eventually got over it.

One other time in Denmark, Emma was on the canal and fell in (with my help). My mark was nearby and I was screaming my wife fell in the canal and couldn't swim (Emma was a very good swimmer). The mark jumped in and I did also. I grab Emma and helped her to the shore and then a lady was pointing to the mark saying he couldn't swim and needed help. I left Emma on the shore and started swimming toward the mark. When I reached him I grabbed him as he was struggling and going under for the second time. We both went under, but only one of us came back up. Me!

During reading my mark's bio I learned where he loved to go fishing on the canal. He was always putting his life in jeopardy for someone else. And that's when I got the idea, after learning that the mark couldn't swim.

I loved those vacations with Emma, even though it was a working vacation. I had no idea she'd stop loving me. But then, Matthew was always around, even though he never worked. I love Emma and I still like Matthew, even though they're having sex together and they did to me what they did. I've killed people for less. Well, that's not true. I've always gotten paid for the people I've killed.

I could forgive them but there is only one little thing; I carry a grudge. I can't help myself. I was in Rome when I first heard about Emma and Matthew. I was researching a hit I was hired to carry out. I had just gone over the bio of this lady, and my employer wanted the job done in three days. I thought I'd take a break and go down to the pub for a cognac and coffee. While I was there sitting on the patio, an associate of mine passed by. He sat down and we started talking about old times. Then the conversation led to Denver and our hometown. He asked me if I was still married to Emma and I said I was, for close to 10 years now. "Why do you ask?"

"Oh, no particular reason," he said. Now, I've been in this business a long time and you know when someone is trying to tell you something. Plus, he and I were in the same line of work and he owed me one.

"Out with it," I said. "What are you trying to tell me?"

He didn't sugarcoat it, he came straight to the point. "Emma and your friend Matthew have been seen together quite a lot, and it hasn't just started. This has been happening every time you go on these trips."

"I get the feeling this isn't just a chance meeting."

"No, it isn't. The company got wind of what's happening and was concerned. They felt once you found out that you would do something irrational and they don't want to lose you."

"Tell the company it'll be all right and I'll handle it. I know you have the location of where they go and when."

In the next couple of days, I finished the job there in Rome and called Emma to say I had to stay another couple weeks, so she would have to get along without me, and to go down to the Lamborghini dealership and pick out that speckled blue one she always wanted.

"Oh, Ben," she said, "you're so good to me. I love you."

"It's the least I can do for my wife after leaving her alone as much as I have. See you in two weeks."

Two days later I was back in the States and in Denver at the Rankin Hotel, Room 1514. At 9:45 p.m. I opened the door to the front room and walked over to the bedroom door. I listened at the door for a good five minutes. Listened to her telling him how much she loved him during lovemaking, and what all she was going to do for him. And all he was saying was, "Yeah baby, yeah baby. And we have two whole weeks of this to go."

"Yes," she said, "it's going to be beautiful. And I'll pick up the car tomorrow; we can go to the beach."

I'd heard enough. I opened the door and naturally they paid me no mind at first. I stood over them as they laid there, both naked, making love. She saw me first and screamed. He raised up and turned to look at me. That's when I hit him, knocking him out of the bed and onto the floor. I also slugged her because she had begun to scream and I wanted to shut her up. I kicked Matt while he was down, in the head, the ribs, and in his groin. And then I repeated the process until I got tired. Throwing him out the window was an afterthought, after looking at them both naked. That's when it really came down on me, really hit me hard. All that I'd done for her, for him.

The rage, I couldn't control it. I had to find release and there was only one way I knew of so I grabbed Matt by his neck while he was still on the floor, groaning. I put my arm under one of his and with one big heave tossed him through the closed window. Emma was half-conscious at this time and saw what I had done. Her mouth fell open without a sound coming out. She knew, deep down, she knew she'd be next.

There was no, "Why did you do it?" from me. No, "I did everything for you." None of that. I just went over to the bed, got on my knees straddling her, and put my hands around her throat and squeezed. Her eyes went wide, hands grabbing at my wrists, but that didn't help her. Nothing helped her.

I informed the company of what I'd done and they immediately put me on a private jet to Taiwan that very night and told me to sit tight. So here I am in this hotel, confessing everything like I'm going to turn myself in. It'll never happen.

Bragging Rights

AMY AND THE girls were having their monthly club meeting and were two hours into it.

"Alex! I'd like to take him on myself but I am president and on Team C." Alex is a virgin, 16 years old, and the girls had made a bet on who would be the one to bust his cherry. The club consisted of 15 girls of high school age. They'd started a club, but not just any club. Their club was to go after nothing but virgins, male virgins. Oh, they still had their boyfriends, but that was completely different than what they had planned. After all, the boys do it all the time, so why not the girls?

None of them were virgins themselves. The game—that's what they called it—worked like this: They found out who the virgins were— and it wasn't as hard as one would think. Sometimes all they had to do was ask their boyfriends, who would be glad to tell them. The other way to find out was to just watch the boys themselves; they just looked like virgins.

The list consisted of five individuals: Alex, 16 and white; Benjamin, 15 and black; Chris, 15 and white; Dion 16 and Puerto Rican; and then there was Duncan, 16 and Mexican. All of these fellows were well known as, for lack of a better word, geeks.

The girls got together in groups of three, giving them five groups. Each group planned to go after one individual. The points they would win depended on their plan. After that, they decided which one of them would have sex with him. If for some reason one of the other girls had sex with him during that same time, that would double their points.

The teams were A, B, C, D, and E. The teams threw names in a hat, and each team member would withdrawal one. After withdrawing their names, each team went to a separate area of the room to put their plan together.

Team A was comprised of Jennifer, Abby, and Alice. They drew Alex's name. Alex excelled at chess, math, and lab. Known as a geek, he also played the clarinet.

Team B was comprised of Maya, Tonya, and Joyce. They drew Dion's name. Dion was a bookworm.

Team C was comprised of Amy, Mabel, and Pearl. They pulled the name of Benjamin. Benjamin was a card collector, Pac-man.

Team D was comprised of Vera, Ruby, and Nettie. They picked Chris's name. Chris loved collecting stamps.

Team E was comprised of Viola, Lucy, and Carrie. They picked Duncan's name. Duncan was a stargazer and astronomer.

Verification would be that one of the other team members would have to witness the event. The winning team would have bragging rights for a month.

The group adjourned until the following month, at which time they would report on their progress.

***

One month later at the girl's clubhouse, Amy called the meeting to order. "We have a lot to go over tonight, so let's get started with Team A."

"We thought we'd get to Alex by learning how to play chess. Alice took the lead on this one and Abby and I just sit back and watch. After a week she was going to his house taking lessons, and after two weeks he was going over to hers. On the third week they went on an official date and went to Lovers Lane and smooched. During that fourth week we felt he was about ready. We informed the other team members for verification. The night before the date, Alex was killed by a hit and run driver."

Team B gave their report.

"Dion spends most of his time at the library so we started there. Tonya took the lead on this one and she met up with him by spilling a Coke on him. After that and a little conversation, she was in. A week of meeting at the library, a hamburger at McDonald's and a movie. Things were going well, and fast. On the third week they were in his basement and making out, but no sex. He informed her he was saving himself for his future wife. After a number of times of making out in the basement, in his bedroom and in his car, Tonya felt she was running out of time. On the last day of the last week, while in Lovers Lane, in the back seat of Dion's car, they made love, but there was no one around to verify it so her conquest turned out to be null and void."

Team C then took the floor.

"Benjamin was our project and he is into collecting cards. There is a storefront that collectors go to. Pearl is a collector (part-time) so we gave her this assignment. Pearl, would you like to tell the group what happened?"

"I met Benjamin at the store and got close to him, and eventually were going out after leaving the store. Since he had no car, we had to make do by going to the park to make out. Amy and Mabel were following me and it had to be awfully boring for them. When we were alone in the park and making out he was on top of me, and all of a sudden he started strangling me. If it wasn't for Amy and Mabel, I don't know what would have happened!"

"You think he was some kind of a nut?" one of the girls asked.

"Well, yeah, don't you think so?"

Team D gave their update.

"Vera, you took this one. What happened?"

As you know, Chris is into stamps, so that's the way I approached him, with a number of stamps I found. Once he got to talking about stamps he wouldn't stop, so eventually I asked him to go for a walk. But he was still talking about stamps on the walk. After a few days of doing this I grabbed his hand and we walked along that way. Pretty soon he talked less about stamps and more about us. On the third week we were at his home sitting on the couch and I kissed him. He grabbed me in a stranglehold and commenced to kiss me back until I told him we couldn't do anything in his house because of his parents. I looked down at his pants and saw that they were wet and he turned around in embarrassment. 'When are we going to get together again?' he asked. 'Soon, very soon,' I said. Two nights later, in the third week, we were in his basement. I had left the side door open for the girls. Once we started making love, the girls came in and watched. Once Benjamin finished with me, one of the other girls grabbed him. In all, Benjamin screwed all of us. We stayed in that basement till two in the morning and plan on going back. Chris, we found, was a needle in a haystack. Put a star by his name."

Viola did the talking for Team E.

"Duncan was the last. Carrie, Lucy and I went after him; he was into the stars. Loves watching Plato, New Ramus, and the Big Dipper. Duncan not only talked the talk but walked the walk. All he ever talked about was the stars, nothing else. He was never known to associate with any girls, so we felt he would be a lot more difficult than the others. We started going by the planetarium and on occasion stopping by his house, where he'd be watching the stars. Carrie took the lead on this one because she's more his type. Small, dark skin, and not so luxurious, but there is something about her that the boys seem to like. She met up with him with one of the oldest tricks around; she slipped and fell in front of him and held her knee like she couldn't get up. Needless to say, he helped her up and asked was there anything he could do for her. One thing led to another, and within the first part of the third week she was in. She found out later that he was true to his stars and hardly touched her until that last week. They were walking home and she took him by way of her house, where she knew no one was there. They ended up on the couch, but after 30 minutes of fooling around he said he had to go. Carrie was pulling his pants down after pulling up her dress and he was getting an erection. When skin met skin, he freaked out… The girls were in the other room and thought they were making love and ran out for their turn. Duncan jumped up after fighting off the girls—and losing most of his clothes—and ran out of the house. Two days later Carrie, Lucy, and I were picked up by the police for assault."

Team D was declared the winner.

Juiced

I was laying on the alley floor behind a dumpster, shooting myself in the neck with heroin. It took me all day to get the money for this shot. I broke in three houses and stole TVs, stereo equipment, jewelry, and money, anything that would sell. I've been on the street now for over three years doing whatever it takes to stay afloat. If I couldn't find money that way, I tried selling my body. I'm still a fairly good-looking woman, although at one time I was told I was beautiful. But this stuff will tear you down over time, mentally and physically. My drug of choice is heroin, of course. I am now what you would call a full-fledged addict. Didn't start out that way.

I started out on weed and then the pills, and just gradually moved up to herein. Before I started using I had it all; nice car, nice apartment, and a good job. My boyfriend was cute as hell and we got along pretty good and I liked him. He was about six foot two and wore nice clothes and all. But once I started using I got him hooked on the stuff, too. He didn't get as bad as me, at first, but eventually he went off the deep end too. But then again, he was trying to keep up with me.

Our relationship went down the tube and he ended up with my best friend. He's been off the stuff for over a year now. I told myself it didn't matter at the time, but it did. She ended up with everything that I used to have, and to tell the truth, I am resentful, but there's not a thing I can do about it. I'd like to say I tried but that wouldn't be true; not very hard, anyway. Maybe a white knight will come by and take me away from all this . . . maybe.

Since I'm feeling a little better, I think I'll go down to McDonald's to their bathroom and try fixing myself up and get ready for tonight. The thing about shooting up is you don't get very hungry; maybe that's why I'm losing so much weight. I've got a backpack where I keep my toiletries and a few clean clothes; dress, sweater, panties, things like that. Don't know what I'll do when winter hits but for right now, I'm good.

I need to make at least $150 tonight; my pusher just went up on his products and he don't take credit. Depending on what the client wants, maybe I can get more than that. And if he lets his guard down, the sky is the limit. I've done that a few times, but only when the client has been inebriated. Most times my action is in a car but there is this motel that charges by the hour; no one wants to go any longer than that. In the three years I've been doing this there has only been two I robbed, and they were from out of town.

I walked into the McDonald's and straight back to the bathroom, took my articles out of my bag and started cleaning up. Ten minutes later I walked out looking like a new woman. Clean face with lipstick, hair combed straight back, dress that reached above the knees and high heels. You would have never known that I had just walked out of an alley.

I walked over to the counter and ordered a cup of coffee, sat down in a booth, and contemplated how I was going to work the night. A couple of young boys came in, got their order, and sat near me. They started giving me the eye and after a few minutes, one of them came over to where I was sitting and said "Goddamn if you don't look good. Is there any chance we could get together?"

"Do you have any money?" I asked.

"Oh, it's like that, is it?"

"Exactly like that," I said. One thing you learn fast on the street is who has and hasn't got it, and who was going to give it up. Certainly not these two.

PART 2

On the street I ran into Bella, who was in the same line of work I was in.

"Much action out here tonight, Bella?" I asked.

"For a Thursday it's kind of dead, but I have managed to make a couple hits. You kind of early; still don't have a place to stay?"

"No," I said. "I'm still at my highrise in the alley. That's getting old."

"Look," Bella said, "my roommate just left, headed back home. Why don't you come stay with me? Won't cost you much, and my roommate's paid up for the week."

"I can go for that. I don't even have to go back to my old place and get my things. You still at the same place?"

"Yeah, I'm still there," Bella said.

"If we lose track of each other tonight and I get there before you I'll wait on the steps. But then again, there'll be no chance of that. I need all the bread I can get so I'll be out here a while."

A vehicle pulled up to the curb and rolled down its window. I walked over to the car and looked in. The person was in his mid-50s with a moustache, bald head, and wearing horn-rimmed glasses and a business suit with vest and pocket watch.

"How much?" he asked. "Depends on what you want," I said. "You know, the usual."

"Usual what?" I asked. "You have to specify."

"The usual sex, no freaky stuff, you know what I'm talking about."

"If I read you right you're talking about the traditional sex, is that right?"

"Yes, that's it, that's what I want."

"That'll be Mr. Jackson, twice."

"I don't understand you, are you saying…"

"Yes, $40."

"That'll work," he said, and I got in the car. "Do you have a place to go?"

"That depends, we can handle this in the car, in which case we can go a few blocks up to an alley. We can go to a motel, in which case you'll have to pay more for the room."

"I'll tell you what," he said. "I think I'd like the motel." An hour and a half later I was back and let out at the same corner where I was picked up. As I was getting out of the car he said, "Thank you."

"Did I hear right?" Bella said. "Did he just say thank you? What the hell did you do to him?"

"You won't believe it, Bella. All he wanted to do was lay in the bed and hold me, that's it. He talked for a while about his wife and kids, that's it. Paid me double what I asked for and as you saw, was very nice about everything. Wish all my tricks were like him."

The next vehicle that pulled up, Bella took. I started walking down the street and occasionally speaking to other girls in the trade. A low ride stopped and a Chicano asked me, "How much?"

"Twenty, twice," I told him.

"Kind of high, isn't it?"

"Depends on what you want," I said.

"For forty bucks I should be able to get an around the world."

"For four times that you can."

"I think I'll pass, this time. Later."

PART 3

It was 2:45 a.m., I felt it was getting late. I had made my quota by $100, but a few more dollars never hurt. As I was on my way towards Bella's place, a 2008 Honda stopped and asked if I was working. I said I was. We determined how much and it was; more than twice what I usually get, so I was more than happy. This had surely been a good night; money, a place to stay . . . yes, this had been a good night. After getting the key from the motel for three hours, we went to the room, removed our clothes and got into bed. He told me to hold on a minute, he had to go to the bathroom. After returning, he had his hands all over me and as always, I played along. Once he got on top of me and I opened my legs I felt something go across my throat; I hardly felt it. I reached up to my throat and felt something wet and sticky. I realized it was blood—my blood. I didn't even have time to panic. I couldn't move and I couldn't breathe. The last thing I felt was the person's weight leaving me. Then my body relaxed and went limp, my eyes got heavy and started to close, and eventually they did.

Of This and That

They said he had the most beautiful eyes they had ever seen. They would just memorize you—and this came from the boys. The girls were dumbstruck too.

He was five foot nine, 160 pounds, blonde hair and turquoise eyes, and one small mole under his left eye. Needless to say, the girls loved him and the boys admired him.

Billy Mayflower was one hell of a young man. He played decent basketball and had fairly good grades in class, but there was just one thing; he dated none of the girls in his school, nor did he associate with any of the guys. No one could figure him out.

Billy was neither stuck up or gay. He went to another part of town and dated other women from there because he had a secret and he wanted to keep it that way. He had no friends, but a number of girlfriends in other parts of town. After the time he spent with his aunt, mostly weekends and holidays, he never dated girls in between. He went on trips around the States and beyond; California, Florida, Canada, Texas, and Mexico. His family had that kind of money. He had no brothers or sisters and his parents stayed on the go, so it was really no problem.

In Florida on spring break, Billy met a girl he really liked, better than any other he had met. She was from Wyoming, a million miles away from El Paso, Texas. And that's the way he liked it. For the week they were in Florida they didn't make love until that last night, and they almost didn't make it then. Velma, the girl's name, was a virgin. She felt she didn't want to give her virginity to anyone back home so she decided on Billy.

On the beach at two in the morning, in a secluded area, they were drinking wine and laying back on a beach towel with a small fire going. During the kissing and caressing, Billy started taking off her bikini. After her clothes were off, she started taking Billy's off and grabbing his penis and feeling around, doing all the things lovers do. All of a sudden she stopped and looked at him and said, "Billy, you're a hermaphrodite!"

On the flight back home, Billy thought about the Velma and that night. Since biology was her best subject in school, it wasn't such a shock to her to find out about him. She took her findings in stride. She even thought it enhanced her first sexual experience. She said she didn't know if she wanted to do it again, but it was an experience she'd never forget. They didn't make any arrangements to ever meet again.

The last week of school and graduation there was one girl he'd always wanted to make love to more than any other, Jamie Lee Bates. She was five foot six, a hundred twenty pounds, red-headed, with blue eyes. She was also the leader of the girls' volleyball and debate teams. Billy knew she liked him, too, so he asked her to go to the graduation ball with him. Needless to say she was surprised and dumbstruck, but she accepted.

Once the other kids heard about Billy asking her to the ball, everyone was talking about it and wondering what had happened to him. One kid was close. He said, "Since this is the last week of the last day of school, Billy just wanted to let it all hang out. I think he has no plans on seeing us again and he seems to like Jamie. Well, we'll soon find out if he's gay or not."

***

After the dance and dinner, they headed for the hotel. At the hotel in the room they opened a bottle of champagne. On the balcony on the 18th floor, they toasted each other and talked about school and why he had been so elusive.

"I promise you, Jamie, before this night is over you will know; you will know it all."

***

At school, while Jamie was cleaning out her locker, a crowd gathered around her and asked was there anything she wanted to tell them. "Well, to set your mind at ease, he's not gay."

"Is that it?" one of the kids asked. "He went through the class year without having sex and that's all? Jamie, are you sure that's all there is to it?"

"That's it, I'm sorry," Jamie said.

Jamie walked out the front door and down the steps of the school. At the bottom, Billy was waiting for her in his convertible Jaguar. She threw her bags in the back and got in.

"Well," Billy said. "Did you tell them all about your adventure last night?"

"Oh, Billy of little faith. I only told them what they wanted to hear, a little bit of this and a little bit of that. Your secret is safe with me."

Predators on the beach

April, 1:15 a.m. It was a Thursday morning. Alex and Carl were cruising the beach, seeing what girl they could find to molest. Each one carried a bottle of wine and had drank a bottle earlier. There was a quarter of a moon out so they could see quite well; the area they were in was very isolated. They had walked so far down the beach until they just dropped.

"I'll tell you what, I'm tired," Carl said. "We sure not going to find no babes down this way. We the only crazy dudes out this far and this late."

"Yeah, I guess you're right. But I sure could use me some pussy right about now. We should have stayed around the motel, at least they had girls there," Alex said.

"Yeah, but who's got time to bullshit them out of some pussy? Takes too long. We catch a woman out here it's wham-bam-thank-you-ma'am. And we out of here."

"Well it looks like we just gonna be left with a hard dick tonight. What you think, should we head back to the motel?"

"Let's rest here a few more minutes and then we can go back, I'm tired."

The boys laid down on the beach and Alex said, "I can see myself right now, me screwing the hell out of this girl. You'd be able to hear her all the way to the motel saying, 'Don't stop, Alex, don't stop.'"

"Well," Carl said, "there are no females out here unless a mermaid comes out of the water."

"The way I feel right now, I'd screw a mermaid," Alex said.

Twenty-five yards down the beach coming toward them were two girls of nineteen and twenty years old, and gay. They were holding hands and kissing, talking about their future. Both were wearing bikinis and a poncho.

At fifteen yards Alex spotted them and said to Carl, "Look what I see. Tell me that's not two girls. Tell me our luck hasn't changed. Hot damn!"

Alex and Carl stayed where they were until the girls were almost on them before they stood up and approached them. "Good evening, ladies, kind of late for you to be out, isn't it? Want some company?" Alex said.

Both girls said no, they didn't want any company, and kept on walking down the beach.

Carl grabbed one girl by the wrist and said, "You may not want any company, but we do."

Alex grabbed the other girl and threw her to the ground, grabbed her around the neck and pulled her over behind some nearby boulders. Alex turned her over on her back and began to pull up her poncho and take her bikini bottoms off.

Meanwhile, Carl was tussling on the sand with the other girl and trying to get her things off. After a few minutes of this, with her bikini bottoms off and her poncho up over her breasts, she wasn't struggling anymore. Carl felt he had things under control. He pulled down his swimming trunks and prepared to enter her…

Twenty minutes later, the two girls were walking back down the beach. Both were cleaning their knives on their ponchos and one said to the other, "About 10 minutes each to take care of them, wouldn't you say? Not bad."

"You know, if they would have gone the other way on the beach we would have had no chance at them. There is always someone back that way. How many does that make now, six, seven? We're getting pretty good."

"I think it's time we moved to another location. What about the parks?"

"We're gonna have to get rid of these ponchos, they're a little too obvious, wouldn't you say?"

"Yeah, but it's a damn good place to hide a weapon. Those boys didn't notice a thing."

Other books by this author:

Enlisted at 14...A Memoir

Enlisted at 14 and the journey continues

Enlisted at 14... Looking back

Willow... A novel

Willow... One for the team

Willow... And the Medusa

Little Miss Willow... A Short Story

Assassin

Meet Ruben Kane

R.K. {Ruben Kane}

Ruben's bag

Ruben's bad side

Smooth...A Ruben Kane novel

Mo Kane

And Then Some

Ducks in a row

Just a dream

Beyond the Curve

Dream Catcher

Blacker the Berry